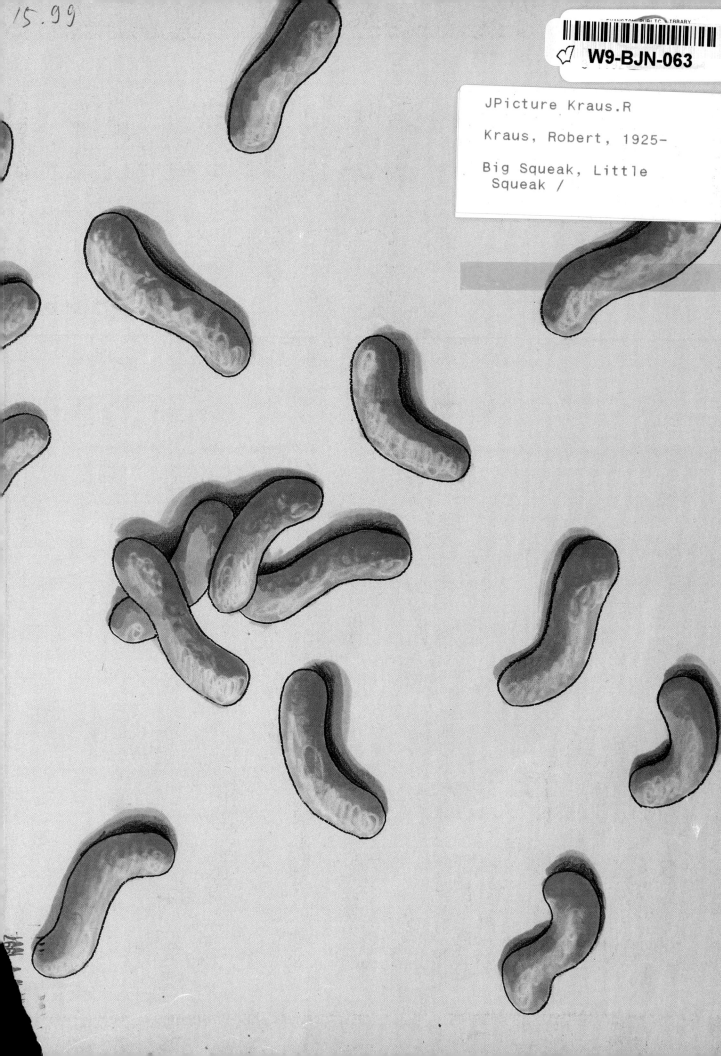

WRITTEN BY
Robert Kraus
PICTURES BY
Kevin O'Malley

ORCHARD BOOKS

New York

Orchard Books • 95 Madison Avenue • New York, NY 10016

Manufactured in the United States of America. Printed by Barton Press, Inc. Bound by Horowitz/Rae. Book design by Jean Krulis. The text of this book is set in 24 point Italia Medium. The illustrations are mixed media on pantone paper.

10 9 8 7 6 5 4 3 2 1

Library of Congress Cataloging-in-Publication Data. Kraus, Robert, date. Big Squeak, Little Squeak / by Robert Kraus ; illustrated by Kevin O'Malley. p.   cm. Summary: Two mice have a dangerous encounter when they venture into a cheese shop run by Mr. Kit Kat. ISBN 0-531-09474-X. — ISBN 0-531-08774-3 (lib. bdg.)   [1. Mice—Fiction. 2. Cats—Fiction.]   I. O'Malley, Kevin, date, ill.   II. Title.   PZ7.K868Bi 1996 [E]—dc20   96-1851

To my grandson, Parker, and to my wife, Pamela—R.K.

To little kids with big squeaks—K.O.

Once there were two mice named
Big Squeak and Little Squeak.
Big Squeak was little but had a big

Squeak.

Little Squeak was big but had a little squeak.

Big Squeak and Little Squeak stayed home all day eating cheese curls and watching mouse cartoons on TV.

"There must be more to life than this,"
said Little Squeak.

"Sure there is," said Big Squeak.

"There's eating real cheese
and watching soap operas!"

So Big Squeak and Little Squeak
went down to the cheese store to shop.
The cheese store was owned
by Mr. Kit Kat,
who found running his shop
a good way to meet mice.
Many mice had gone into his store,
but none had ever come out.

In walked Big Squeak and Little Squeak.
"How can I help you mice?" asked Mr. Kit Kat,
rubbing his paws together.
"We'd like some cheese," said Little Squeak.

"And I'd like a nice plump mouse,"
said Mr. Kit Kat,
grabbing Little Squeak by the tail.

"Help!" squeaked Little Squeak.
Into a hole in a big Swiss cheese
jumped Big Squeak.
How could he save Little Squeak?
How could he save himself?
Then he got an idea.

FREE

"This is the big cheese talking,"
he said in his loudest voice.
"Drop that mouse or I'll fill you full of holes!"
"A talking cheese?" said Mr. Kit Kat.
"I've been in this store too long."
Mr. Kit Kat dropped Little Squeak
and ran screaming from the store.

Big Squeak and Little Squeak let all the mice
out of the traps in the basement,
where Mr. Kit Kat had been saving them
for a feast.
Then they threw a party for all the freed mice.

You can bet there was a whole lot
of squeaking going on.

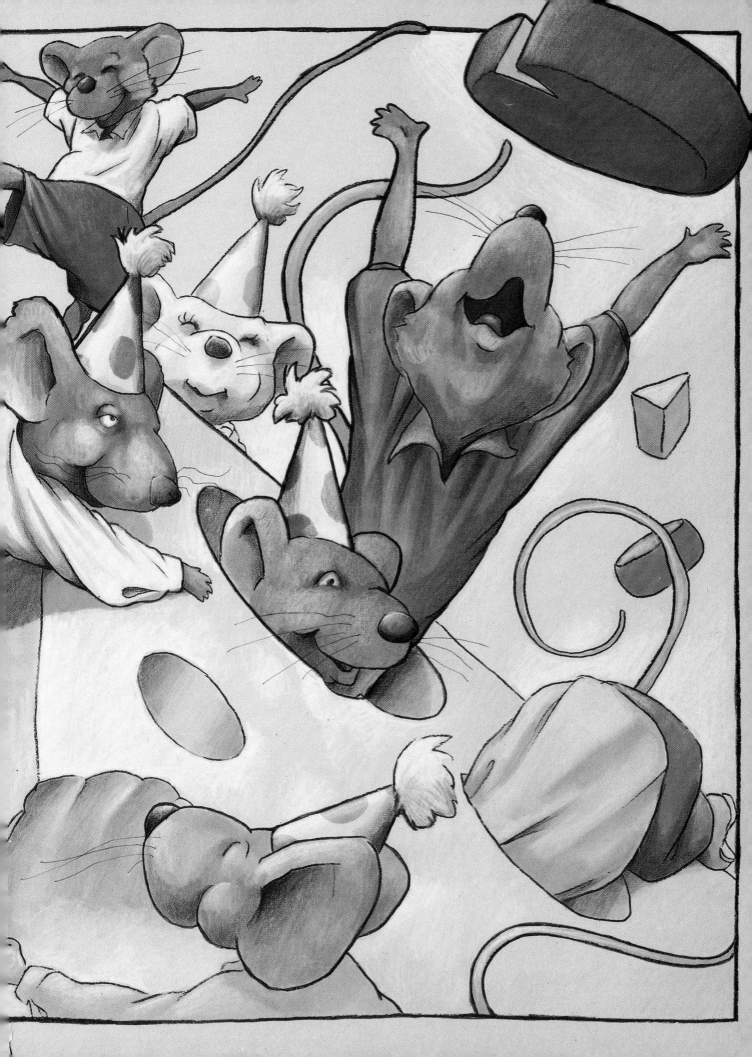

And Mr. Kit Kat was never seen again.
Not even a whisker!

FREE
FISH

Mr.
Woof's
Woofs